Rich in Mercy

personal testimony
of Linda Schubert

Other Books by Linda Schubert

Miracle Hour
Precious Power
True Confessions
Miracle Moments
The Healing Power of a Father's Blessing
Five Minute Miracles

Revised Second Printing — February 2005

Scripture references are from the New International
Version unless otherwise noted.

Linda Schubert
Miracles of the Heart Ministries
P.O. Box 4034
Santa Clara, CA 95056
phone/fax (408) 734-8663

Rich in Mercy

"Because of His great love for us, God, who is rich in mercy, made us alive with Christ..." (Eph 2:4-5).

One thousand people were seated on folding chairs in the church parking lot in Lagos and storm clouds were gathering. I was in Nigeria as a speaker for the 23-year celebration of charismatic renewal in that country. Halfway through my talk on forgiveness the rains came. The enthusiastic Nigerians didn't seem to mind; they were used to greater hardships than getting soaked in the pouring rain.

Later that evening I thought about the struggles and hardships of these people, and my own inadequacy in the face of overwhelming needs. "Lord," I cried, "The needs are so great and I am so little!" His reply stole my heart: "Little in My hands is much." I cried out, "Then help me get it into Your hands!"

I've shared this story many times in my travels around the world, along with the word from the Lord that first took me to Nigeria. But before I tell how I managed to go to West Africa, I'd like to share some of the wonders of God's love in taking a girl who had walked down so many wrong paths, and setting her on the Royal Road. My story is a message of hope, especially for those who feel their soul will never sing again. It's a story of encouragement for those who feel God can't possibly have any use for them, because of past failures. **Lord, You are rich in mercy. Let your mercy pour out through these pages and into the hearts of every reader. Please anoint these words and the eyes and ears and hearts that receive the words. Let Your Spirit rise up through the words and accomplish Your great and wonderful purposes. Amen.**

My early childhood years were spent on my grandmother's 2400-acre ranch high up in the Santa Lucia mountain range along the Northern California coast between Monterey and Big Sur. My grandmother, Florence Hogue, was a pioneer schoolteacher who came to California from Chicago in a covered wagon and developed a reputation in transforming unruly coast boys into responsible citizens. My early education was in a one-room school on the coast with 15 students, six grades in one room.

Dad, Charlie Vander Ploeg, was an atheist and the son of generations of Dutch atheists. He was deeply resistant to the word of God. Mom had encountered Christ as a student at San Jose State College in California, but because of the difficult family dynamics, my sister, Cherrill, and I were not raised in a Christian home. My only "catechism" growing up was the little children's song, "Jesus loves me." There were many sunny afternoons on a rope swing hanging from an ancient oak tree, when I would push high into the trees, back and forth, singing, "Jesus loves me, this I know, for the Bible tells me so. Little ones to Him belong, they are weak, but He is strong. Yes, Jesus loves me, Yes, Jesus loves me, Yes, Jesus loves me, the Bible tells me so." Seeds of God's love were being planted in my heart by Jesus Himself, through that anointed little song.

As a child and into my adulthood I was afraid of men. I could not open my spirit and feel free with them. There was an invisible wall. The family considered me a wild child; everyone was afraid I would turn out like Aunt Ruth. I worked hard to live up to the reputation! Aunt Ruth was definitely the family black sheep, a renegade newspaper reporter and photographer with an unconventional life-style. In today's world she'd fit in pretty well.

When I was 19, and a student at San Jose State, I met and married Bill. Abandoned by his father as a child, our marriage triggered in him a desire to locate the father he had never known. After an intense search, he made a call one day to a man in Atlanta, Georgia. "I believe I am your son," he said to the stranger. He quit college and left for Atlanta. I sold my grandmother's treasured piano for travel money and followed my husband in his quest for roots.

After a few months of trying to make it work and failing, with heavy hearts we boarded a train for California. We were traveling on Easter Sunday in the late 1950's across the Texas plains. Bill and I had been drinking in the club car and found a hidden room for some loving, when the train screeched to a halt. What I saw outside the window left a permanent scar on my soul. The train had crossed a bridge over a deep river canyon, where families were picnicking together. Six children were walking across the railroad bridge when our train came upon them. One jumped, and broke his leg in the fall. Pieces of five young bodies were strewn in the dry grass outside the windows of the train, as families watched in horror from below. That day I made a vow to never have children. Something died inside.

As I look back, I'm convinced I went into an emotional breakdown. Shortly after our return to California I ran away and left Bill, and obtained a fast Reno divorce. (Twenty-five years later I learned that the man from Atlanta was not Bill's father after all.) A few weeks after the divorce was final I married Dick, a boyfriend from high school days. A year later I ran away from him, too. By the time I was 23 I had been married and divorced twice. Life was in a downward spiral, spinning wildly out of control. I had no sense of how to build a productive life; I just didn't know how to live.

When I was in my mid-twenties, I met and married Ron, a divorced man with four children.

The children came to live with us when they were six, eight, ten and twelve. Shortly after their arrival, Ron told the family that he wanted us all to become Catholic. We made an appointment with Father Dermody at Our Lady of the Rosary parish in Palo Alto, California. He carefully studied our marital history, then explained that in order to become Catholics we would have to live the rest of our lives as brother and sister, rather than as a married couple. While our decision to accept this ruling shocked those who heard the story, it became for me a grace, especially in the later years when I knew that for emotional survival I needed a measure of distance from Ron.

Instruction in the Catholic faith was exactly what I needed. I learned about the God of history and our heavenly Father's wonderful love plan to restore people to fellowship with Him. I learned about the life, death and resurrection of Jesus; I learned about the ministry of the Holy Spirit. Through this process, the Lord was bringing order out of the chaos of my life. Christian education has enormous potential.

Yet my Christianity was still head knowledge; it had not yet reached my heart. As with so many other people, the Lord gained my heart through personal crisis. My third stepson, Randy, was diagnosed with a rare untreatable cancer, and died at age 21. A week after he died I turned on my television one day to a Christian evangelist I had never heard before. Pat Robertson on the 700 Club was inviting listeners to surrender their lives to Jesus. Falling to my knees I prayed with him, something like this: **"Jesus, I am so sorry for the way I have lived my life. I repent of all the wrong choices, and all the wrong paths. I turn from those wrong paths and I turn to you. Please come into my life and be my Savior and my Lord. I give my life to You. Please fill me with Your Holy Spirit. Amen."**

In the preparation classes I had learned about the person and the work of Jesus. On this historic day, I took the next step. I said, **"Jesus, knowing who You are and what You have done for me, I now give my life to You."** I could tangibly feel the presence of the Holy Spirit, loving me, filling me with His life. I climbed into our old Dodge van and just drove around, windows wide open, singing in the Spirit from the depths of my soul. This was the beginning of a journey of discovering how our Lord takes amazing responsibility for our lives when we entrust them into His care.

The next morning I looked out the door of our home in San Jose, California, and something was radically different. I said, almost to the wind, "I don't have any friends." I had lived my life to that point completely closed off from other people. I had not shared the deep pain in my heart with even one other person. Now I realized I couldn't live like that anymore. When the Holy Spirit comes, He is a God of community. He calls us to come together, to help each other grow in love. So I spoke out, standing at the door, **"Lord, GIVE ME FRIENDS."** It was in our move to Springfield, Virginia, the following month, that He answered this prayer.

In Holy Spirit parish in Springfield after daily Mass one morning, I literally fell into the arms of Mary Augusta Roseberry, a little gray haired lady who became my first friend. We would go to her home after Mass and have coffee, and talk. Little by little, she heard my whole story. Piece by piece, I let down my barriers. Her warm, safe unconditional love soaked into my bruised and broken spirit, bringing freedom and hope. I came to know the wonders of God's mercy through her compassionate love. She was a reflection of the heart of Jesus.

While the period following Randy's death was a time of resurrection for me, it was a time of collapse for other family members. My second stepson became schizophrenic, and my husband had a nervous breakdown. Later on, my step-daughter had a massive stroke and was confined to a wheelchair. In retrospect, I feel if we had all done some healthy grief work, things might have been different. But I look with hope to Romans 8:28: *"And we know that in all things God works for the good of those who love Him, who have been called according to His purpose."*

We returned to California, a 3,000-mile drive with a sick husband in the front passenger seat and Coffee, a 16-year-old dying Siamese cat, in the back seat. Shortly after our return home

Coffee died. I cried more tears for that cat than I had cried for anything else in the past few years. His death was an opportunity to release years of old uncried tears. The Lord was doing a deep healing in my life.

Scripture became my daily food. I would read my Bible for hours and hours at a time, sometimes into the late hours of the night. My spirit was coming alive. I was beginning to hear the voice of God in my spirit. The Lord says, *"My sheep listen to My voice; I know them, and they follow Me"* (Jn 10:27). He would speak in my spirit, in my thoughts, in my mind. One of the earliest scriptures that was significant to me was Deuteronomy 30:19-20, *"I have set before you life and death....Now choose life, so that you and your children may live and that you may love the Lord your God, listen to His voice, and hold fast to Him. For the Lord is your life...."*

Sometime during this period of awakening, I came to understand that the fear of men that had imprisoned me, was rooted first in childhood sexual issues connected with my father, and also with men close to the family. As I say this, I want to make it clear that I do honor my father, as will be evident later in the story. I just wasn't safe in his arms. He would touch girls in a way that wasn't fatherly. I began to pray that sometime before he died, the Lord would bring healing between myself and my father. In the years to come I would often pray that prayer.

Another moment of deep conversion came in 1984 when I was diagnosed with breast cancer. By then I was a strong Christian, and my friends would look at me and say, "You're strong, Linda, you can handle this." Truthfully, I was scared to death. My grandmother had died of breast cancer, and my mother had a mastectomy a few years before my diagnosis. Breast cancer ran in the family.

At this point I need to admit that all of my life I had been basically a selfish person, turned inward upon myself. We all have areas where God deals with us. This was one of my issues. Matthew 6:33 became a focus of serious prayer: *"Seek first His kingdom and His righteousness, and all these things will be given to you."* The Lord continually invited me to take my attention off myself and look to the needs of others.

My last night in the hospital following the mastectomy, the Lord spoke to my heart: "I want you to go in and pray for the man in the next room." My instant response was typical of my old nature: "I'm feeling sorry for myself, Lord. Send someone to pray for me instead." The Lord had frequently sent people to pray for me! Finally, after shameful resistance, I got up, put on my robe and slippers, and went to the door of the man's room. He was a handsome black man in his mid-thirties with a bandage over his eyes.

By this time I had been trained in hospital visitation procedures, and knew there was an appropriate protocol in approaching patients. But

I did not follow the rules. I tiptoed over to his bed, leaned over and whispered: "The Lord sent me to pray for you." In the silence that followed I could see tears trickling down his cheeks. Then he spoke: "Today I gave my life to the Lord, and today I learned that I would never see again. You can't know how much your coming in here means to me." He had been blinded by a gunshot. The presence of the Lord flooded the room. The blind man knew that God had heard his prayers, and the healing for me was just as powerful. I don't remember the words I prayed, but by that time it just didn't matter. God was present in a powerful way.

When I returned to my room I fell to my knees and said, **"God, I'm so sorry for being so selfish and self-centered. I don't know how much time I have left in this life, because I know that breast cancer is tricky, but I make a vow to You today to make every moment count in the kingdom of God. With Your grace, when You say, 'Who will go for Me?' I will say, 'Here I am, send me.' "**

Upon returning home I bought a world map and put it on the wall, where it became my place of prayer. Almost blissfully I would place my hands on different countries and continents and say, "I will go wherever You want me to go, Lord." Sometimes I would say, "Send me to places where no one else wants to go." Within six months I began writing for Rev. Robert DeGrandis, S.S.J., and spent the next five years coauthoring nine books with him--popular books that have been translated into many languages. At the time I thought this was the fulfillment of the map prayer; later I would see that it was just the beginning.

But I want to refer back to my mother and father, particularly to the time when Dad was in his early seventies and a retired building contractor in Northern California. Mom was then a practicing Christian and working as a special education teacher in Marysville, California. One day Dad announced to Mom that he had joined a weekend nudist colony. She was horrified. "What will my friends think?" she moaned. "You can join me," was his flippant response. She was humiliated, and deeply ashamed. Then one day it got even worse. He met a woman at the nudist colony and decided to run away with her to Guadalajara, Mexico. My parents had been married more than 40 years. Hang-in-there years, tough but faithful. While they were miles apart intellectually and spiritually, there was a good friendship between them.

God's grace was with Mom as he announced his decision to leave. She tearfully washed and ironed his clothes, bought food for his camper truck, and got him all ready for his "grand adventure." When he climbed into the truck to head south, they faced each other in tears. "I just have to do this," he mumbled, and drove off.

In the days and weeks to come, Mom discovered something interesting. She realized it was really quite nice around the house without Charlie. "I can go to lunch with my friends," she reflected. "I can go to Bible studies." And again, "It really is quite nice around the house without Charlie."

Have you ever been going about your every-day business when you feel the presence of the Lord, as if He wants to say something? One day in her office Mom sensed the strong, gentle voice of the Lord: "Elizabeth, what do you really want?" That's an extremely important question for each of us. Have you heard the Lord ask you what you really want? I believe He wants us in touch with the desires of our hearts. If we go deep enough, beneath our casual self-focused desires, we may discover our deepest desires are the Lord's own desires for us. The following experience taught me something about this issue.

One day I was in the Old City in Jerusalem, wandering through the shops looking for something to buy. Nothing was appealing. In a moment of frustration I said, "Lord, find me something I really want!" Moments later I found myself in a little shop with ceramics and hand-blown glass. A turquoise blue candle holder caught my eye. Holding it gently, I turned it over and read the gold and black label: "Hebron glass." I whispered, "Oh, Jesus." Only the Lord knew that the one place I had longed to go on that particular trip (but couldn't) was Hebron, where Abraham and the old patriarchs were buried. In that holy moment in the tourist shop in Jerusalem, the Lord took me to Hebron in my heart. He revealed a desire of my heart, and answered it perfectly, in His way.

As Elizabeth pondered the Lord's question, her response rose from the deepest place in her soul: **"Oh Lord, I really want a marriage."** His response was infinitely tender: "Loving Charlie is My choice for you. It's what I want you to do with your life." At that moment she knew herself and she knew her God. And all she could do was lay her life at the foot of the cross. She laid it down with self-knowledge; with clarity and charity, with love and total surrender. She accepted the truth of Galatians 2:20: *"I have been crucified with Christ and I no longer live, but Christ lives in me. The life I live in the body, I live by faith in the Son of God, who loved me and gave Himself for me."*

Doesn't Dad seem like a "senior citizen prodigal son" of the story in Luke 15? Remember how the prodigal went off to the distant land and squandered his life, found himself in miserable circumstances, and had a change of heart? Not long after Mom's conversation with Jesus, Dad was in an automobile accident in Guadalajara. A carload of young men hit his camper truck broadside and it overturned. Apparently it tipped over ever so gently, almost as if angels laid it on its side. For some unknown reason, Dad landed in a Guadalajara jail. He was extremely miserable. In his misery all of his values mysteriously cleared up, and when he was released from jail he ran home to Mom, leaving the other woman behind.

Again, God's grace was with her, because she received Dad with open arms and open heart. He was still an atheist, and came home with more bad habits than he left with. She spent the next five years just loving Charlie. Day by day by day by day. One afternoon she was ready to give up. It was just too hard. The Lord knows those exact moments when we are about to make decisions. As she thought about packing her bags and leaving, the Lord spoke again, tender and clear: "Elizabeth, you have to learn it sometime, it might as well be now!" "Learn what, Lord?" she asked. "Do you want to love Charlie?" She nodded. "Then love him with My love. Do you want to forgive Charlie? Take My forgiveness. All of My resources are yours. I'm here to be your life and ability. Come, take, receive."

That's when Mom learned how to pray in power. She discovered that in her weakness and inability, all she had to do was step aside, inside, and let the Lord's life flow through her to be her love, forgiveness, strength and wisdom. Sometimes in the early morning she would get up and open her Bible to 1 Corinthians 13:4-8: *"Love is patient, love is kind. It does not envy, it does not boast, it is not proud. It is not rude, it is not self-seeking, it is not easily angered, it keeps no record of wrongs....It always protects, always trusts, always hopes, always perseveres....Love never fails."* In time, after soaking in it over and over, that portion of scripture came alive in her. She could say, "God's love in me is patient, and kind. God's love in me keeps no record of wrong...." *"For the word of God is living and active. Sharper than any double-edged sword, it penetrates even to dividing soul and spirit, joints and marrow; it judges the thoughts and attitudes of the heart"* (Heb 4:12).

When my father was 80 years old he was paralyzed in bed with a stroke. One day he called out, "Elizabeth, I need help." She misunderstood and said, "Charlie, I'm doing this...I'm doing that..." He persisted, "You don't understand, I need help!" At that moment my sister, Cherrill, walked into the house and the whole scene was a reenactment of a dream she had a week before. She walked over, knelt down at his bed and asked, "Daddy, would you like to receive Jesus?" "Yes, of course," he responded. Cherrill said later, "It was so easy." It was so easy because of all those years of loving that melted down generations of tough, Dutch atheism. Melted in the love of God.

Dad was totally healed. He could get up, he could use his walker, he could get back to his favorite chair in the living room. We had five more years of loving Charlie the Christian. From that moment on, every prayer Mom prayed for him was answered. When he had a fever she would touch his forehead in prayer and the fever would leave. He would fall, and a strong man would appear at the door to get him back in his chair. Sometimes people would come and sit in the living room and just soak in the awesome presence of God's love. One day Dad looked up and saw an angel at his right shoulder. "I'm not ready to go," he cried out. The angel left.

When he was 85 he was truly dying. As I flew to San Diego where they were then living, I reminded the Lord of my prayer of so many years. "Lord, he's in a coma, and it's too late for the healing of our relationship." His response was firm: "With Me it is never too late."

The time alone in his room was precious. Praying quietly, I remembered a time on the mountain when I was eight years old. Dad's leg had been crushed in a terrible logging accident. When I arrived home from school that day I saw visible evidence of the nightmare in the imprint of a blood-soaked hand on the back of a man's shirt. Many years went by, and that image would return, with the emotional trauma associated with it. Then one day when I was resting in prayer, I saw the image again. But something was different. Jesus entered the picture, walked over, and placed His own nail-scarred hand over the bloody imprint. Then after a few moments, He removed His hand. The bloody imprint was gone. Jesus had taken it to Himself, along with all the traumatic feelings. I was left with a peaceful memory, safely enclosed in God's love.

As I sat beside my father on his deathbed, crying out to God for healing in this relationship,

I sensed the holy presence of Jesus once more. Then my father spoke two words; they shot out like bullets from a high-powered rifle, yet a person in the room would not have heard a whisper. He said, "I'm SORRRRRRYYYY!" The words traveled some 40 years back to a hurt little girl, and something came to rest inside. I said softly, "I forgive you Daddy." The next day my father died. Jesus had taken him to Himself.

In the days and weeks to come I discovered that a lot of my old fear of men was beginning to leave. For the first time in my life I found that I could begin to develop warm open friendships with men as brothers. It was a wonderful healing.

All of my life I've run away from close relationships with men. It's hard for me to admit my three marriage failures; it's a terrible record. But I'm learning to accept God's forgiveness and I'm learning to face pain and not instantly run away at the first sign of trouble.

God is love (1 Jn 4:16). He is calling us to be like Him. So He will face us with issues of loving and invite us to allow Him to love through us. As we pray, we are being conformed to His love nature. And He is saying, "Come. Take Me by the hand. Let Me take you through the pain. Let Me be what you need. Let Me teach you how to love, because I am Love."

A woman called me one time and told me some things about her life. She had been born with a serious blood disease and was not expected to live. But her parents stood beside her and taught her how to deal with pain. "Face the pain honey," they would say. "Face the pain with your eyes on Jesus. Don't run away from it, don't hide from the difficulty. Walk through it with your eyes on Jesus."

The Lord wants us to look to Him and allow His life to grow in the midst of all the pain in our lives, physical and emotional and spiritual. He wants us to trust Him with our circumstances. He wants us so surrendered and connected to Him that whatever challenges we face, we will turn to Him trustfully and say, "How do You want me to respond to this, Lord? How should I feel about that?" He would have us so utterly given over to Him that we make room for His Spirit to rise in us through the situations in our lives.

As I write this I am remembering the song I was silently singing to Jesus at Mass one morning, "Let Your Spirit rise in me." Throughout that day I sang, "Let Your Spirit rise through my confusion...let Your Spirit rise through my weaknesses...let Your Spirit rise through my thoughts ...Oh Jesus! let Your Spirit rise!"

A year or so after my father's death, I was on a plane flying from San Francisco to New Orleans, when I saw a bright and shining image of his face. The Lord said to me, "Now receive back into yourself the goodness of your father." Because of hurts of the past, I had shut everything about him out of my life. And when I opened the door in my heart and let his goodness back in, something deep and wonderful came to rest.

On another occasion I was driving past a house where we had lived as a child, and old painful memories came to mind. I heard in my heart the compassionate love of Jesus: "Linda, your father didn't know how to love; he didn't know how to do things right; he just didn't know how." Because I had made a decision in my heart to honor my father, I was able to hear the Lord's voice concerning my relationship with Dad. *"Honor your father and mother...that it may go well with you..."* (Eph 6:2).

My mother, Elizabeth Joy Vander Ploeg, died of heart disease in 1995. In her final hours she said to me, "Linda, always remember Philippians 4:19: *'My God shall supply all your needs according to His riches in glory.'*" She said, "Never forget that, Linda." I replied, "I will remember, Mom." Then she asked for a back rub. A few days later as I sat beside her hospital bed, I asked for her blessing. She reached out and touched my forehead with love, and said a prayer of blessing. Those were her final words to me.

On the day after her funeral I was sitting alone in Mom's little cottage in the Oregon woods, making a fire in her wood stove and running my hands over the arm of her favorite chair. I started to speak to Jesus, and it came out in song: "Lord, I don't want her to be gone, I miss her so much." Again, there was His wonderful presence. In the silence His voice slipped from heaven into my soul, in tune with my song: "What if you knew how happy she was?" All I could do was worship Him.

After her funeral I flew to the Island of Malta in the Mediterranean, to keep a speaking engagement to open the first meeting of the Magnificat Ministry to Catholic Women in Europe, and to grieve with dear friends, Myriam and Richard England. They took me to the Maltese Island of Gozo for a few days, where we walked and talked and ate and slept and saw some beautiful places that Mom would have loved. Then I learned that Gozo meant "Island of Joy." Mom's middle name. "Lord, You are so good." While in Malta I prayed with my dear friend Madeleine O'Connell's father, Baron Jerome de Piro D'Amico Inguanez. He died shortly after Mom died, also of heart disease. The Lord was so good to us as friends, sharing our grief and praying together. Surely our parents have met in heaven!

After Mom's death, my sister and I decided it was time to take a trip together. In all of our growing up years, we never had a family vacation--ever. For many people this would seem incomprehensible, but for our family, living was just an ongoing struggle for survival. A huge fire destroyed our ranch on the California coast when I was 12, and we moved from town to town throughout California following construction jobs. I have stark memories of living in dusty little trailer camps in desert towns, then moving on and never planting roots. Life was hard, and we were poor.

So Cherrill and I flew to Toronto, first class, using up all of my accumulated first class upgrades as a platinum American Airlines passenger. It was good fun. We talked about life, her children, prayer, my travels, and the value of tambourines in praise and worship.

One evening on our trip I was flooded with images of our childhood ranch as rolling hills and valleys of dry grass. As I shared the picture with my sister, we were both in touch with the emptiness and lack of nurturing in our childhood. Then I thought about all of my own difficulties in developing a productive healthy life, and saw with new clarity how my sister had the same struggles. I had always assumed life was easier for her because she was such a responsible older sister, and now a compassionate hospice nurse. She was never the rebellious black sheep like her younger sister. Yet I discovered in many ways we were more alike than different. A new love and appreciation for her began to settle into my heart. We also shared the love and appreciation we felt for our parents, who struggled so hard to make things work. We extended forgiveness and blessing to them, and made a commitment to stay connected.

After Mom died I found her prayer journal in a bedside stand, and began to study her private reflections. It was amazing. The fears and insecurities and self-preoccupation that I have struggled with could have easily been hers. And her deep thirst to really know Jesus, her continually going to Him with searching questions, could have been mine. Here are a few gems from her journal:

* "The Lord makes it plain in His word and in my interaction with Him that He honors us with strength and a quiet spirit when He is worshipped and praised."

* "The word the Lord has given me since Charlie died is 'through.' He has taken me 'through' many rough times. It's not my earth-to-heaven relationship that bothers me, it's the earth relationship loneliness. I want to go 'through' this with Him to victory."

* "Yesterday I came across a discussion of God's rest in the Amplified Bible. It's ease, I think. Relief from anxiety; refreshing; God's rest. It involves a relationship with Him. His yoke gives rest to our souls. Meditate on the truth of God's word until you settle into His rest. It makes sense at last."

* "I didn't realize that the problems that have been plaguing me for so long are strongholds I need to ask the Lord to break. Remnants of self-pity; feelings of not belonging. I want Him to break the strongholds."

* "I found this in the Living Bible, Isaiah 7:9: *'If you want Me to protect you, you must learn to believe what I say.'*"

* "Self-pity times must be kicked aside and the Lord's wisdom received. It's hard to face ourselves, sometimes, yet we must if living is to be vital. And I do want a walk with the Lord

that is real and vital. Not religious in the
wrong way. Real, and clean."
* "I've wasted a lot of time feeling sorry for myself."

What really stands out about Mom's life, especially in her later, fully Christian years, is her
trust in Jesus. Seeing the thread of trust woven
through her life, growing ever stronger, is so precious. In her writing I could see the Holy Spirit
at work in a yielded woman, still insecure and
fearful in some ways, but God's special treasure.
A precious heritage.

Now back to the Lagos story. Once during a
speaking tour in Alaska, I was in a log cabin in
Juneau participating in a prayer meeting with
Christian leaders. During the praise time a
woman spoke: "There is someone here holding a
door closed that the Lord wants open." Something rose up deep inside me and I blurted out,
"Oh it's me. I don't want to go to Africa." In
front of these leaders I repented, and invited the
Lord to open that door. I had not consciously
said, "Lord, I don't want to go to Africa," but
when the subject of Africa was in front of me, I
found myself unconsciously turning away. It was
a big unknown, and I was afraid to trust in Him.

Trust is a key issue. During prayer one time I
asked the Lord, "How have I offended You today?" His answer was swift, "You still don't trust
Me." Shocked, I said, "In what way, Lord?" Another swift reply, "In health and finances." He

gave me a panoramic view of how He had cared for me over the years. He reminded me of the time He saved the life of my mother and me when she was ten months pregnant with me, with serious complications. He revealed many times throughout the years when He lovingly cared for me in spite of my turning away and not heeding His voice. The subject of trust is a big issue, not only in me, but in people everywhere I go. At this writing I've spoken to groups in more than 15 countries, and we are so much alike in this area of trust. I think this is a signal to look at the relationship with Jesus. If there is closeness and intimacy, a deep relationship, trust will eventually conquer old hurts that are barriers to trust.

But back to Juneau, Alaska. All of this happened in the month of May. In July of that same year I received a phone call in the middle of the night from Victor, a prayer group leader in Lagos, Nigeria. And so I went, except that my surrender was still not complete. I was in the Detroit airport following a weekend of ministry, with tickets from Detroit to London to Lagos. And I was coming down with a cold, and I was exhausted. I called Pat Mullins, my prayer group leader, and said: "Pat, I'm sitting in the Detroit airport, heading for Lagos, and I'm getting a cold. I don't want to go to Africa, I want to go home and go to bed!" Oh, the body of Christ is so precious. Pat went to battle for me, as I curled up in the phone booth, 2000 miles away. He came against the enemy, he commanded the illness to leave, he reminded me that Jesus is my life and the Holy Spirit poured God's life back into me. I felt like a warrior again. Oh, the power and privilege of interceding for brothers and sisters in the body of Christ.

I've told a little bit of what happened in Lagos. Our little in God's hands is so much more than we can appreciate. A little mustard seed, a word here, a prayer there. In His hands it will be good, even if we never know the fruit of simple, faithful obedient steps. What is so special is how the Lord works with us, never forcing, but inviting us closer. He continues to stand at the door and knock, longing for intimate involvement in our lives. He continues to say, "I will be for you what you need Me to be."

Perhaps as you read this, the Holy Spirit is showing you a door that is not yet open to Him. Will you give Him permission to walk through that door? Are you afraid to trust Him? Are you afraid He will send you to Africa? (May I tell you that going to Nigeria was the most precious trip I have ever taken? The people were wonderful. I learned so much. I fell in love with them! And what if I had kept the door closed? Oh, look what I would have missed!)

Pray with me: **Lord, in Your great mercy let Your Spirit rise up through our muddled lives, through the hidden hurts and the failures and the losses. Let Your Spirit rise up through the places in us** that are not well. Jesus, we give our lives to You! Bring us to wholeness, in body, soul and spirit. Bring us to wholeness in relationship with You, and with each other. We thank You, we praise You, we worship You. Give us a living and vital relationship with You--not religious in the wrong way, but real, and clean. And let us, along with Elizabeth, not waste any more time feeling sorry for ourselves. Let us focus all our energy on living every moment for You, allowing Jesus to live His life in us. We love You heavenly Father; we love You, Jesus; we love You, Holy Spirit. Amen.

"I pray that out of His glorious riches He may strengthen you with power through His Spirit in your inner being, so that Christ may dwell in your hearts through faith. And I pray that you, being rooted and established in love, may have power, together with all the saints, to grasp how wide and long and high and deep is the love of Christ, and to know this love that surpasses knowledge --that you may be filled to the measure of all the fullness of God" (Eph 3:16-19).

When people ask me about my story, I often comment that it is always changing. How true for all of us. But what I wanted to add to the story are a couple of things. First, just to say that the Lord has been healing me in a lot of the areas of trauma, including the terrible train wreck on page four. Looking back, I probably suffered from a post traumatic stress disorder that kept me bound. A lot of healing work has been accomplished in that area. The story of my father running away with another woman to Mexico has had ongoing amazing events in my life. I traveled to Guadalajara, and the Lord sovereignly opened the door for me to pray with prisoners in that jail. And enroute to the jail, pray with dying twins in a hospital, and share God's love on radio that broadcast through central Mexico. (Including sharing a song inspired in a dark time of my life.) The twin Mexican babies were healed, and many other blessings flowed, and continue to flow. The childhood desolation on page 21 is turning to fruitfulness. And the Lord has blessed my praying with babies. When I asked Him about that, He responded, "I never gave you any children of your own, so I am making it up to you." So much love! My website www.linda-schubert.com often has more updates.

One final update is that I am a widow now. Ronald died in April 1999 from an overdose of his psych medicine. He loved the Lord very much, but his thinking was pretty distorted. So we leave that in the Lord's hands. The Lord knew his heart.

Order Form

To order Linda Schubert's books and tapes, send with payment in U.S. funds to Linda Schubert, Miracles of the Heart Ministries, P.O. Box 4034, Santa Clara, CA 95056; phone/fax (408) 734-8663.

Books

___	*Rich in Mercy* (Linda's testimony) $2.00	___
___	*Precious Power* $2.00	___
___	*Miracle Hour** $2.00	___
___	*Healing Power of a Father's Blessing* $3.00	___
___	*Miracle Moments* $2.00	___
___	*Five Minute Miracles*** $4.95	___

CD's

___	Miracle Hour prayers .... $ 8.00	___
___	Double CD Miracle Hour Teachings & Prayers $14.00	___
___	Receive the Gift (Linda's song sung in English and Spanish .... $ 8.00	___

Scripture Focus Tape Series

___	strength $4.00	___
___	trust $4.00	___
___	peace $4.00	___
___	prayer $4.00	___
___	healing $4.00	___
___	worship $4.00	___
___	hope $4.00	___
___	joy $4.00	___
___	wisdom $4.00	___
___	mercy $4.00	___

Total $ _____
California residents add 8% tax $ _____
Shipping*** $ _____
TOTAL ENCLOSED $ _____

Ship to _____

_____

_____

Phone _____

*For quantity discount of *Miracle Hour,* use the following chart:

1-25 copies	$2.00 each
26-50 copies	1.75 each
51-99 copies	1.50 each
100+ copies	1.35 each

**Bookstores order *Five Minute Miracles* from publisher, Catholic Book Publishing, 77 West End Road, Totowa, NJ 07512 (973) 890-2400. For other books, standard trade discount applies.

***For shipping to U.S. locations, refer to chart below:

1 to 5 items add $2.00
6 to 20 items add $3.00
21 to 35 items add $4.00
36 to 50 items add $5.00
51 to 70 items add $6.00
71 to 99 items add $7.00
100 items add $8.00

To Canada double the U.S. shipping cost and send payment in U.S. FUNDS. For shipping to other countries, write for cost.

If you are interested in having Linda come to your area for conferences, retreats, workshops or healing services, write or phone:

Linda Schubert
Miracles of the Heart Ministries
P.O. Box 4034, Santa Clara, CA 95056

Phone/Fax (408) 734-8663
email linda@linda-schubert.com
www.linda-schubert.com